Kids

The Sound of K

By Alice K. Flanagan

The Child's World®, Inc.

K

Kindergarten kids have lots of fun.

Kids will do all kinds
of things.

Kids learn numbers one to ten.

Some kids write with
a pen.

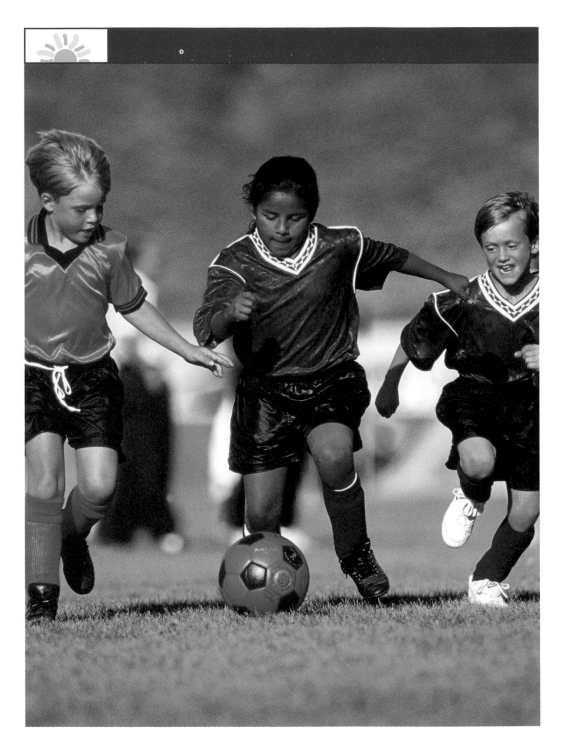

Some kids kick and toss a ball.

Some kids run and do not fall.

Some kids dress up like a king.

Some kids dance, and some kids sing.

Kindergarten kids have lots of fun.

Kids will do all kinds
of things!

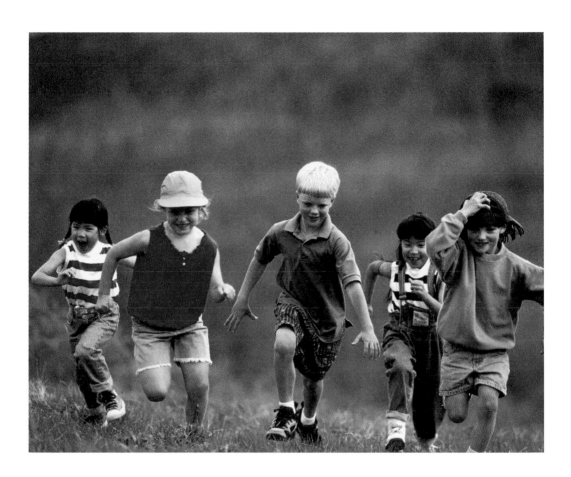

Word List

kick

kids

kindergarten

kinds

king

Note to Parents and Educators

The books in the Phonics series of the Wonder Books are based on current research which supports the idea that our brains are pattern detectors rather than rules appliers. This means children learn to read easier when they are taught the familiar spelling patterns found in English. As children encounter more complex words, they have greater success in figuring out these words by using the spelling patterns.

Throughout the 35 books, the texts provide the reader with the opportunity to practice and apply knowledge of the sounds in natural language. The 10 books on the long and short vowels introduce the sounds using familiar onsets and rimes, or spelling patterns, for reinforcement. For example, the word "cat" might be used to present the short "a" sound, with the letter "c" being the onset and "-at" being the rime. This approach provides practice and reinforcement of the short "a" sound, as there are many familiar words made with the "-at" rime.

The 21 consonants and the 4 blends ("ch," "sh," "th," and "wh") use many of these same rimes. The letter(s) before the vowel in a word are considered the onset. Changing the onset allows the consonant books in the series to maintain the practice and reinforcement of the rimes. The repeated use of a word or phrase reinforces the target sound.

The number on the spine of each book facilitates arranging the books in the order that children acquire each sound. The books can also be arranged into groups of long vowels, short vowels, consonants, and blends. All the books in each grouping have their numbers printed in the same color on the spine. The books can be grouped and regrouped easily and quickly, depending on the teacher's needs.

The stories and accompanying photographs in this series are based on time-honored concepts in children's literature: Well-written, engaging texts and colorful, high-quality photographs combine to produce books that children want to read again and again.

Dr. Peg Ballard
Minnesota State University, Mankato

Photo Credits

All photos © copyright: PhotoEdit: 2 (David Young-Wolff), 17 (Rudi Von Briel); Romie Flanagan/Flanagan Publishing Services: 5, 6, 8, 18; Tony Stone Images: 10 and 21 (Lori Adamski Peek), 13 (Dugald Bremner), 14 and cover (Rosanne Olson).

Special thanks to the Fahrenbach family

Photo Research: Alice Flanagan
Design and production: Herman Adler Design Group

Library of Congress Cataloging-in-Publication Data

Flanagan, Alice K.
    Kids : the sound of "k" / by Alice K. Flanagan.
        p. cm. — (Wonder books)
    Summary : Simple text and repetition of the letter "k" help readers learn how to use this sound.
    ISBN 1-56766-709-0 (lib. bdg. : alk. paper)
    [1. Kindergarten Fiction . 2. Alphabet. 3. Stories in rhyme.] I. Title.
    II. Series: Wonder books (Chanhassen, Minn.)
PZ8.3.F6365Ki   1999
[E]—dc21
                                99-20959
                                CIP